Twister
A Terrifying Tale of Superstorms
By Samone Bos

LONDON, NEW YORK, MUNICH,
MELBOURNE, and DELHI

DK LONDON
Series Editor Deborah Lock
Project Editor Camilla Gersh
Project Art Editor Hoa Luc
Producers, Pre-production
Francesca Wardell, Vikki Nousiainen

DK DELHI
Editor Pomona Zaheer
Assistant Art Editor Tanvi Nathyal
DTP Designers Anita Yadav, Vijay Kandwal
Picture Researcher Sakshi Saluja
Dy. Managing Editor Soma B. Chowdhury

Reading Consultant
Shirley Bickler

First published in Great Britain by
Dorling Kindersley Limited
80 Strand, London, WC2R 0RL

Copyright © 2014 Dorling Kindersley Limited
A Penguin Random House Company
10 9 8 7 6 5 4 3 2 1
001—253404—June/2014

A CIP catalogue record for this book is available
from the British Library.

ISBN: 978-1-40935-194-8

Printed and bound in China by South China Printing Co., Ltd.

The publisher would like to thank the following for their kind permission to reproduce their photographs:
(Key: a-above; b-below/bottom; c-center; f-far; l-left; r-right; t-top)
1 Corbis: Mike Hollingshead/Science Faction. 6 Dreamstime.com: Mylightscapes (tl). 7 Alamy Images: Lightworks Media (br).
8 Alamy Images: Ian Cartwright travel (tl). 10 Corbis: Ashley Cooper (bl). 12 Alamy Images: incamerastock (tl).
14 Alamy Images: Roger Coulam (bl). 16 NOAA: (tl). 16–17 Dreamstime.com: Liubirong. 17 Alamy Images: RGB Ventures
LLC dba SuperStock (tl). 18–19 Dreamstime.com: Christoph Weihs (Frames). 20 Alamy Images: Hugh Threlfall (br).
Dreamstime.com: Empire331 (br/Maps); Stephen Vanhorn (br/GPS). 20–21 Dreamstime.com: Antos777.
21 Dreamstime.com: Steven Cukrov (cb); Ronald Van Der Beek (bc); Hpphoto (bl). 22 Alamy Images: Mylightscapes (tl).
24 Alamy Images: Ryan McGinnis (tl). 29 Alamy Images: December Blvd Photography (tl). 38 Dreamstime.com:
Mylightscapes (tl). 39 Alamy Images: David Mabe (r). 43 Alamy Images: JohanH (tr/Frame); Tatiana Morozova (tr). 44–45
Dreamstime.com: Linas Lebeliunas (Frame). 46–47 Getty Images: Martin Lladó (tl). 48–49 Getty Images: Wild Horizon/UIG
(t). 50 Getty Images: sandsun/E+ (bl); Mike Theiss/National Geographic (cl). 50–51 Alamy Images: Stocktrek Images, Inc.
(c). Getty Images: Manuel Sulzer/Cultura (bc). 51 Getty Images: Cultura Science/Jason Persoff Stormdoctor (cr). NOAA: (br).
52–53 NOAA. 56 Dreamstime.com: Mylightscapes (tl). 59 Alamy Images: Ryan McGinnis (br). 61 Alamy Images: Roger
Coulam (br). 63 Alamy Images: Ivan Montero (br). 65 Alamy Images: Mark Romesser (br). 67 NOAA: (tl, tr, cl, cr, bl, br).
68 Alamy Images: Ryan McGinnis (cl, br). 69 Alamy Images: Ryan McGinnis (tr). Corbis: Jim Edds/Jim Reed Photography
(tl); Jim Edds (bl); Jim Reed (br). 70–71 Dreamstime.com: Tanatat (Frame). DVIDS: NASA. 71 Alamy Images: Dennis
MacDonald (cb). 74 Dreamstime.com: Mylightscapes (tl). 75 Alamy Images: Jana Thompson (br). 77 Alamy Images: Roger
Coulam (b). 78 Alamy Images: Terry Smith Images (br). 80–81 Alamy Images: Craig Ruttle (b). 82 Alamy Images: Patrick
Sahar (b). 86 NOAA: (cl, bl, br). 87 NOAA: (tl, tr). Science Photo Library: Howard Bluestein (br). 88 Dreamstime.com:
Mylightscapes (tl). 90 Alamy Images: A. T. Willett (b). 93 Getty Images: Carsten Peter/National Geographic (b). 94 Getty
Images: Steven Hunt (l). 96–97 Alamy Images: WoodyStock. 99 Getty Images: Brett Deering. 100 Corbis: Warren Faidley
(c). 105 Alamy Images: Franck Fotos (cla); Q-Images (tl); Andre Jenny (bl). Dorling Kindersley: Mid-America All-Indian
Center Museum, Wichita,Kansas (clb). 106 Dreamstime.com: Mylightscapes (tl); Darko Sreckovic (br). 108 Alamy Images:
AF archive (t). 111 Alamy Images: Stocktrek Images,Inc. 113 Getty Images: Nick Caloyianis/National Geographic.
114–115 Getty Images: Erik Simonsen (t). 116–117 Corbis: Warren Faidley. 123 Corbis: Warren Faidley (br).
Jacket images: Front: Getty Images: John Lund/The Image Bank (t), Ryan McGinnis/Flickr (b);
Back: Alamy Images: WoodyStock (t)

All other images © Dorling Kindersley

For further information see: www.dkimages.com

Discover more at
www.dk.com

Contents

Tornado Alley

Welcome to Tornado Alley! This is an area in the central United States of America (USA) that is regularly hit by tornadoes. It includes parts of Oklahoma, Kansas and Texas.

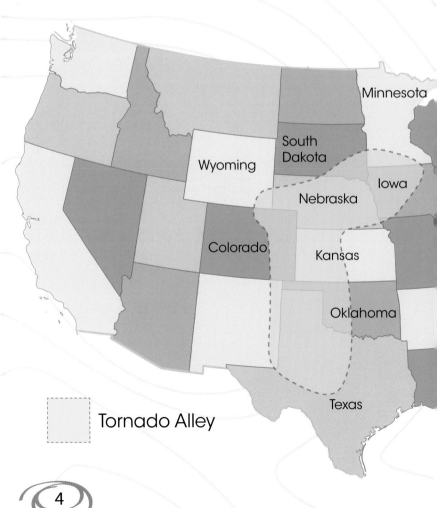

Tornado Alley

Tornado facts

The 31 May, 2013, El Reno Tornado was the widest ever, peaking at 4.2 km (2.6 miles).

The 18 March, 1925, Tri-State Tornado covered 352 km (219 miles) in 3½ hours.

The 27 April, 2011, outbreak had the most tornadoes in 24 hours, with 209 twisters.

From 21 to 23 November, 1992, there was the longest continuous tornado outbreak ever – 94 tornadoes struck in 54 hours.

The USA is hit by an average of 1,253 tornadoes per year.

CHAPTER 1

A Bumpy Arrival

Jeremy could not believe his luck – bad luck, that is.

It started with the hot dog he ate for lunch. The menu gave it the big thumbs-up: 'Chef's #1 favourite! Flame-grilled wienerwurst served with sweet Bavarian mustard, tangy slow-roasted ketchup and a seedy wholegrain bun'.

'Seedy' was one way to describe it.

Jeremy had frowned at the sad, grey sausage slathered in red and yellow gloop, but he ate it anyway. Now he was 10,000 metres in the air and stuck on an aeroplane toilet with tummy troubles. Passengers kept banging on the door.

"Hurry up in there!"

"Did you fall into the toilet, kid?"

"Don't you people have any manners?" snapped Jeremy. "I am suffering from an unfortunate case of hot dog poisoning."

"So call a doctor!" someone whined. "I need a wee."

Jeremy's luck went from bad to worse when the plane started lurching in the sky. Ding! Ding! Ding! Ding! The fasten-seatbelts alarm bleated. Perched over a swirling toilet bowl, Jeremy tried not to panic.

"This is your captain speaking," a voice boomed over the speaker. "We are experiencing a little turbulence, due to a severe thunderstorm passing through

Oklahoma City. Please fasten your seatbelts and, uh, enjoy the ride."

"Enjoy the ride?" Jeremy groaned. "On a toilet?" He looked around. There were no seatbelts. The plane was bound to crash, and he would be discovered sitting on the loo.

He imagined what the TV reporter would say: "The boy is a genius! Wrapping his body in loo roll while the plane plummeted to the ground saved his life." Jeremy would probably win awards for his Loo Roll Crash-Landing Survival Technique, but he would never live it down at school. His stomach was still doing somersaults, but he had to get out of the toilet. Now.

As Jeremy washed his hands, the plane rolled to the right. A wave of soapy water crashed down the front of his light-grey jeans – more bad luck.

Jeremy opened the toilet door. The angry mob was gone. A flight attendant, strapped in a jump seat, looked very angry.

"Sit down!" he hissed.

Trying to hide wet trousers and walk in a yo-yoing plane was tricky. Jeremy lurched down the aisle like a soggy Frankenstein monster. Finally, he sat down.

He leafed through the airline magazine and read 'Some Fun Facts about Oklahoma City'.

'Fact! Oklahoma City has more tornado strikes than any other city in the USA.

Fact! Oklahoma City's Will Rogers World Airport is named after America's favourite cowboy.

Fact! Will Rogers tragically died in a plane crash in 1935'.

Jeremy gulped. Clunk. Clunk. Clunk. Was something falling off the plane? CLUNK. Jeremy squealed! Everyone on the plane turned and laughed at the squealing teenager.

"Crew, prepare cabin for landing," came the captain's calm, confident and deep voice.

Humiliated, Jeremy shrank back and tried to relax. First, he imagined fluffy clouds. Then an imaginary thunderbolt zigzagged out of those clouds and struck the plane.

Zaaaaaaaap! Jeremy squeezed his eyes shut for the entire landing. He much preferred taking the bus.

Jeremy grabbed his bag and wandered through customs. He braced himself for the worst luck of all: a dreary holiday with cousins he had never met.

When his parents announced their second honeymoon in tropical Fiji, Jeremy dug out his snorkel and flippers. Then Jeremy found out he was not invited. Worst of all, his cousins were meteorologists. Who wanted to drone on about the weather all day? People did that enough back home in London.

No, Jeremy would show zero interest in meteorology. He would spend the next week reading books, watching TV and minding his own business.

He dawdled to the greeting area and scanned the waiting crowd.

"Over here, Jeremy!" came a pair of excited voices.

He saw his twin cousins Jack and Flash Ryder running through the terminal. They looked like their pictures. Jack high-fived Jeremy and Flash gave him a warm hug.

"Airport security guards were inspecting our van," Flash explained, as she tried to catch her breath.

"Well, it does look a little… odd," Jack chuckled mysteriously.

Puzzled, Jeremy followed his cousins out of the terminal and through the busy multi-level parking lot.

"So, how was the flight?" asked Jack. Now that his stomach had calmed down, Jeremy decided to keep the suspect hot dog to himself. He also thought it best not to mention his squealing.

"Not bad," he lied. "Well, I spilled water everywhere," he added, pointing at the hoodie tied around his waist.

"Urgh, I always do that!" groaned Flash. She waved ahead at a large van, with security guards eyeing it curiously. "That's our ride," she announced.

This was no ordinary van – it was heavy duty. A cluster of aerials and other devices sprouted from the roof like quills on a porcupine. Through the windows, he could see that it was bursting with equipment.

Jack reached into the van and pulled out a trucker cap with some words in sprawling graffiti letters on it: 'Ryders on the Storm: Jack and Flash Ryder. Storm Chasers!'

Jack raised his eyebrows at his cousin.

"Did your parents mention that Flash and I like to chase storms?" he asked.

Suddenly, Jeremy was more interested in the weather.

Ryders' Scrapbook

THE DAILY STORM
18 September, 1989

HUGO MIRACLE TWINS!
Babies Born During Hurricane!

Our stormy arrival!

A storm is born!

SCIENCE TODAY
5 January, 1995

Researchers Take on Groundbreaking Tornado Origins Study

Nebraska News
23 MAY, 2004

Hallam Tornado Was 4 Km Wide

The most super supercell of them all!

THE LONE STAR ★
24 DECEMBER, 2009

Rare Blizzard Strikes West Texas

Santa brings snow to Texas!

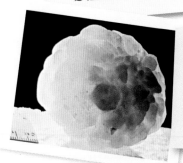

THE NATIONAL
24 July, 2010

LARGEST-EVER HAILSTONE FOUND IN SOUTH DAKOTA

THE TUMBLEWEED
15 SEPTEMBER, 2012

Central Great Plains Drought Worst Since Dust Bowl

Bone dry!

Dust as far as the eye could see!

THE OKIE
18 OCTOBER, 2012

Interstate 35 Closed Because of Dust Storm

THE NATIONAL
28 May, 2013

Storm Chaser Captures Footage from Inside Tornado

In a whirl!

Storm Chasers!

Storm chasing has a long history. It has greatly contributed to our understanding of tornadoes. Here are a few storm-chasing pioneers.

Neil B. Ward was the first storm chaser who was also a scientist. He worked for the National Severe Storms Laboratory, and he is best known for having created a tornado in his home laboratory.

Tetsuya 'Ted' Fujita was a pioneering tornado researcher. Known to some as 'Mr Tornado', Fujita developed the Fujita Scale, which measures how severe a tornado is.

David K. Hoadley is a photographer and the world's first storm chaser. He began as a teenager, and in 1977, he founded the magazine *Stormtrack*, a forum for storm chasers around the world.

Sean Casey is a filmmaker and storm chaser, best known for his role on the documentary series, *Storm Chasers*. He built the Tornado Intercept Vehicles, two stormproof trucks with IMAX cameras.

Storm-chasing Gear

Storm chasers carry a range of equipment.
Sometimes they carry just a few basics.
Other times, they carry advanced instruments.
Here are a few essentials.

1. Laptop
This helps storm chasers combine all the data that has been collected.

2. Maps
If something happens to the GPS, storm chasers need a back-up plan.

3. GPS
The Global Positioning System (GPS) helps storm chasers find their way from one storm to the next quickly.

4. Mobile phone
This is needed to keep in touch with the weather station or for emergencies.

6. Radio
This helps to keep up with weather alerts and stay in touch in an emergency.

5. Food and drink
These are needed in case storm chasers take shelter during a storm.

7. Digital camera
Storm chasers need good cameras so they can take lots of pictures.

No Ordinary Visit

As they hurtled away from the airport, Jeremy's mind whirred. Did his parents know that Jack and Flash were storm chasers? Everywhere he looked, electrical cables curled like serpents inside the van. There were computers, cameras, radios, headphones and strange technical equipment he did not recognise.

Jeremy frowned.

"Isn't storm chasing dangerous?" he asked. Flash caught Jeremy's gaze in the rearview mirror and smiled.

"Dude, 'Danger' is my middle name!" she replied.

"Is it?" asked Jeremy uncertainly. Her first name was 'Flash', after all!

"Flash's middle name is Florence," laughed Jack, shaking his head.

"It can be very dangerous," Flash replied, suddenly serious, "but we are professional meteorologists. We constantly monitor the situation."

"Is that what this equipment is for?" Jeremy asked. "Monitoring storms?"

"These are the tools of our trade," Jack explained. "Some of the equipment is for our work at the National Weather Service. One day, we'll have a fleet of support crew for Ryders on the Storm. We'll make use of those radios!"

Jeremy eyed the jumble of devices. Did they really need that much stuff to see if it was raining out?

"What do you know about Oklahoma?" Jack quizzed.

"I heard something about a tornado alley." Jeremy yawned. The journey from the United Kingdom had taken 17 hours. With no direct flights from London, he'd had to change planes, with a long layover in Houston, Texas. "Is that like a bowling alley?" Jeremy continued.

Flash chuckled. "Bowling alley! Well, Tornado Alley is a large expanse of the central States that is prone to tornado strikes. There is no official zone, but the alley generally scoots between the Rockies and the Appalachian Mountains."

"Slow down, Flash!" Jack interrupted. He motioned out the window. "Jeremy, look to your right. Oklahoma is famous for its dome-shaped schools."

Jeremy spied some peculiar round structures. They looked like fungi.

"That school is built to withstand tornadoes," Jack continued. "Many Okies have tornado shelters, but some public buildings – such as that school – are pretty much stormproof."

"Your house is stormproof, right?" Jeremy asked, suddenly concerned.

"No, not stormproof," Jack shrugged. "We've made it storm-friendly, though: hurricane clips; reinforced, bolted doors; shuttered windows – the best we can do."

A few minutes later, Flash pulled into the driveway of a neat, brick house. Two labradors barked happily, meeting them at the front door.

"Sonic! Hedgehog! Meet your cousin, Jeremy," said Flash, ruffling their shiny coats.

Jeremy patted the friendly pooches.

"I've got two black cats named Toil and Trouble – something from Shakespeare," he grinned. "Mum thinks they have got a sixth sense."

"Psychic cats!" exclaimed Jack, waving his hands in the air. "Do they read paws?"

"Well, they dash under the sofa just before anyone rings the doorbell. Do your dogs do anything like that with the weird weather around here?"

Flash rubbed her temple thoughtfully.

"There are theories that some animals may hear something called infrasound before a big storm or earthquake strikes," she explained. "It's sound that's inaudible to humans."

"We always have the animals taken care of in bad weather, though," Jack interrupted. "Anyway, enough talk about storms. Come in for some pie!"

Jeremy breathed a sigh of relief. He was famished. He followed his cousins inside. This pie had better be good!

QUESTION:
What questions would you want to ask Jack about tornado strikes?

Jeremy gobbled three slices of peach pie.

"If only pie were this good at home!" he groaned.

Jack dropped a jar of pickled fruit on the table.

Someone had written "Bunker crop! Peach!" in swirly orange letters.

"Bunker?" Jeremy repeated. "Shouldn't it say 'bumper', as in 'huge' or 'splendid'?"

Flash stood at the door holding two enormous torches.

"Follow me, Jeremy!" she beckoned. "This will make things clear."

She led her cousin down a concrete path away from the house. Sonic and Hedgehog bounded ahead. They barked at a trapdoor angled in the ground. Flash lifted the trapdoor. She handed Jeremy a torch.

Jeremy followed her down the narrow stairwell. In the low light, he spied a mattress, blankets, a first aid kit and a radio.

"I'm sleeping here?" he asked nervously. "Underground?"

"No!" hooted Flash. "Welcome to our storm cellar: the Bunker. It's our refuge whenever a tornado strikes. It's also where we store our preserved fruit."

Jeremy then noticed the wall of jars.

"Phew!" he sighed. "I thought I was in a real jam."

That night, Jeremy had freaky dreams: pie-eating contests, psychic pets, tornadoes.

In the morning, sunlight crept through the curtains, warming his face.

"Rise and shine, kiddo!" Flash sang through the door. "Pancakes are ready!"

Pancakes? Jeremy snapped awake. In the kitchen, he found hot chocolate, berries, peaches and juice. This wasn't breakfast. It was break*feast*!

Jack poured the maple syrup. "What do you usually do on holiday?" he quizzed. "Visit the zoo? Museums?"

"Yeah," Jeremy shrugged. "I go on all sorts of excursions."

"All sorts of excursions," Jack repeated, chuckling under his breath.

"Have you unpacked yet?" Flash asked, spearing pancakes on her fork.

"Not yet," Jeremy replied.

"Good," Jack nodded. "Put your bag back in the van."

Jeremy gulped. "Is something wrong?" he asked.

"Not quite," Jack replied cryptically.

He handed his cousin a trucker-style cap. It was the same kind with graffiti writing that Jack had been wearing yesterday: 'Ryders on the Storm'.

"You, little cousin, are our newest storm chaser!" he cheered, slapping Jeremy on the back. "We're leaving in 45 minutes."

Jeremy's stomach flip-flopped. This was no ordinary visit.

What is a Storm Shelter?

A storm shelter is a structure designed to protect people from tornado-strength winds and flying debris. It can be underneath a house, a room in the house or a separate building.

Walls are made of a combination of plywood to absorb shock, and steel to resist wind pressure.

The structure is separated from other buildings so that damage to these buildings will not affect the storm shelter.

SECURING YOUR HOME

1. Tornado winds can tear the roof off a house. Secure the roof with braces or straps.

2. Protect the windows of your home from flying debris by installing storm shutters or nailing plywood to the outside.

3. Install additional stormproof bolts on the doors. Garage doors can be secured with braces.

Ventilation duct prevents pressure from building up in the room, which could cause collapse.

Steel door closes securely with three deadbolts.

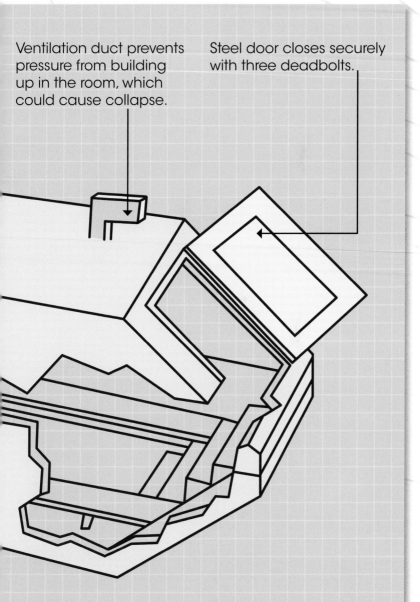

Tornado Survival Tips

If you are ever caught in a tornado or severe storm, it is important to know what to do and how to act to ensure that you and your family get through it safely.

1. Gather together an emergency kit with enough food, water and other supplies (such as batteries and a first aid kit) to last for 72 hours.

2. Prepare a family communications plan: how to get to a safe place, how to contact one another, how to get back together and what to do in different situations.

3. Listen to local weather forecasts, and be aware of danger signs, such as a dark sky or large hail.

4. If you are under a tornado warning, seek shelter immediately in a pre-designated shelter, usually a basement, a storm cellar or the lowest level of a building.

5. Remain in your storm shelter until the danger has passed.

6. Leave the shelter carefully, always being aware of hazards such as flooding, falling debris, collapsing buildings and blocked roads.

7. Check for injuries that anyone might have received during the storm. Seek treatment for minor injuries and medical attention for more serious injuries.

Blueberry Pancakes

Sometimes called hotcakes or flapjacks, pancakes are perfect for breakfast and easy to make. Eat them with butter or smother them with maple syrup.

Makes 12 pancakes
Preparation: 10 minutes
Cooking: 15 minutes

150 g (1¼ cups) flour
1 tbsp baking powder
½ tsp salt
1¼ tsp caster sugar
230 ml (1 cup) milk
1 egg
½ tbsp melted butter
75 g (½ cup) blueberries

1 Sift the flour, baking powder, salt and sugar into a large bowl. Lightly beat the milk and egg together in a small bowl.

2 Pour the milk mixture into the flour mixture. Mix in the butter. Let the batter stand for one hour.

3 Heat a non-stick frying pan over a medium heat, and add a little butter. Add a large spoonful of batter to the pan, or as many as you can fit, depending on the size of the pan.

4 Sprinkle a few blueberries over the surface. Cook the pancakes until the tops begin to bubble, and they are golden underneath. Flip them over and cook until golden, and each pancake has risen to about 1 cm (½ in.) thick.

5 Repeat until all the batter is used up. For a real treat, serve with maple syrup.

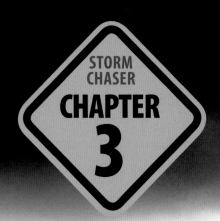

Chasing the Target

Flash and Jeremy bundled sleeping bags into the van.

"I hope you dig prehistory, kid, because we're stepping back in time to Dinosaur Valley, Texas," Flash explained. "A severe storm is expected this afternoon."

A grin slid across Jeremy's face. Dinosaur Valley sounded awesome.

"You cross state lines just to see storms?" he asked.

"We are nerds like that," Flash replied cheerfully. "In the morning, we consult

the Doppler radar and set our target. Then we drive till we hit it."

"What's the Doppler radar?" Jeremy asked.

"See that tall structure over there, with a giant white ball on top? Inside is the Doppler radar. It tells us how fast weather systems are moving and what direction they're moving in so we can predict where storm systems will be," Flash explained.

Jeremy nodded in comprehension.

Jack strolled out with Sonic and Hedgehog. He had a gym bag brimming with balls from various sports.

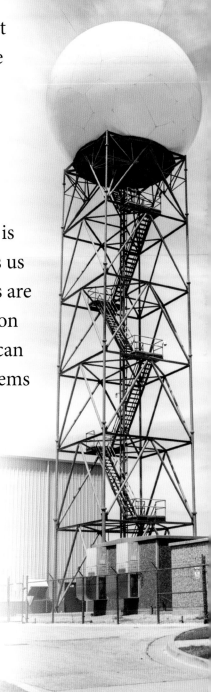

"Are these guys coming, too?" Jeremy asked, ruffling Hedgehog's black coat.

"Oh no!" Jack replied. "I'm taking them to our neighbour, Katie."

"And you give them *all* those balls to play with?" Jeremy asked, his eyes bulging.

Jack shook his head. "The balls are coming with us!"

After saying farewell to the dogs, Jeremy sat in the back seat as Jack and Flash checked the van and technical equipment.

"Map? Where's the map?" Jack insisted.

"Uh, don't you have about fifty GPS devices?" Jeremy suggested.

"We've got a few, kid, but in an emergency, nothing replaces paper!"

Soon they were off on Interstate 35. Jeremy lounged back and almost started enjoying his cousins' deafening – and slightly embarrassing – taste in classic rock music.

"I hope you're strapped in there!" Flash shouted above the din, which was mostly Jack singing.

"Of course!" replied Jeremy. Then she swerved abruptly towards an exit ramp.

"Just got two more pickups!" she explained.

A few minutes later, Flash pulled into a suburban driveway. A young man and woman waved excitedly at the van. Silver trunks lay at their feet.

The man flung the door open.

"G'day mate!" he said, shaking Jeremy's hand. "I'm Barney from Australia."

"And I'm Suze!" added the woman, also shaking Jeremy's hand. "I'm from San Francisco."

Jeremy's ride suddenly got even more crowded. Barrelling along the plains, Jeremy learned that Suze was a photographer and Barney was a filmmaker.

They, along with the van's six mounted webcams, documented their storm chase every spring.

The storm chasers rounded a bend near Denton, Texas. Suze leaned forwards. "Flash!" she blurted. "Pull over!"

As Suze scrambled out, Jeremy hid under his cap. Was she car sick? Vomit churned up his stomach!

"Gross," he gurgled.

Barney elbowed him in the ribs. "Relax, mate! Suze collects clouds."

Sure enough, Suze had her camera angled at the sky.

"Oh." Jeremy shrugged, eyeing the billowing cloud. It looked like an enormous mushroom.

Jeremy was intrigued by Suze's photos.

"Which clouds do you collect?" he asked.

She passed him a tablet device. Jeremy scrolled through folders with familiar names from the weather report: cirrus, altostratus,

altocumulus, stratus, cumulus and cumulonimbus.

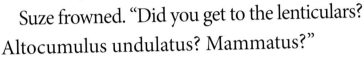

"Impressive," he observed politely.

Suze frowned. "Did you get to the lenticulars? Altocumulus undulatus? Mammatus?"

Jeremy looked again. There were albums of clouds that looked like UFOs, stripes and – freakiest of all – cow udders.

"Whoah!" he marvelled, no longer faking.

"That cloud is a cumulonimbus incus," Jack explained. "It's anvil-shaped and can grow into a..."

Barney yelped excitedly.

"GUYS!" he interjected, jabbing his mobile. "Dinosaur Valley is old news. We've got a much bigger beast."

QUESTION:
Look up at the sky. How would you describe the types of clouds you see?

43

Cloud Spotting

Clouds are named according to appearance. Here are a few types.

Cirrocumulus
Occurring at high altitude, cirrocumulus appears as thin sheets or layers.

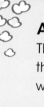

Altocumulus
This is a mid-level cloud that forms rolls arranged in waves, or rounded masses.

Stratus
This is a low cloud that forms a featureless, grey layer covering the sky.

Stratocumulus
This forms patches of white or grey cloud.

Cirrus
Cirrus clouds are the most common type of high-level cloud. Winds can draw out these clouds into wisps.

Altostratus
This mid-level cloud appears as a grey or slightly blue sheet of cloud.

Cumulus
These are low, fleecy, white and separate from each other, with blue sky in between.

Cumulonimbus
This dark, low cloud is the type that causes thunderstorms and tornadoes.

Jack and Flash swung around to listen. Barney handed Flash the mobile. "Look, there's severe storm activity forming west of Paris on the Doppler radar," he elaborated. "I'll check the GPS for the precise spot."

"We're worried about storms in France?" Jeremy groaned.

"Paris, TEXAS!" everyone shouted.

Suze clambered back into the van. Flash took the next exit east.

"Barometric pressure down," Jack announced a while later.

"What does that mean?" Jeremy asked.

"Barometric pressure is sort of like the weight of the air. When the pressure

is down – that is, when the air is lighter –
it means that there are a lot of clouds and
a lot of moisture in the air. In other words,
it's when thunderstorms can happen."

After two hours, the sky shimmered
with electricity. Barney's camera rolled.

"Intra-cloud lightning, Jeremy!" explained
Jack. "IC between you and me."

Jeremy glanced ahead. Right before them,
a blue lightning bolt skewered the ground.
Thunder gave it a round of applause.
CRAAAAKOWWWW! Jeremy squealed.

"Meet cloud-to-ground lightning!"
laughed Jack. "Sneaks up on you, doesn't it?"

Flash parked in a clearing. She grinned
at Jeremy in the rearview mirror.

"Twenty kilometres southwest of Paris," she announced. "Welcome to the city of lights!"

The storm chasers monitored their computers, checking radars and anemometer readings. Jeremy puzzled over some of the equipment. "What does that do?" he asked, pointing at a device that looked like a sideways windmill.

"That's an anemometer. It measures wind speed," Flash explained.

Jeremy eyed the lightning-charged sky nervously. "Isn't it dangerous to use electrical equipment?" he asked.

"We're on battery power," Jack explained. "Just don't touch the van's frame."

"She's spectacular, but a standard multicell cluster," Flash informed Suze and Barney. "Let's sit tight until the squall lines pass."

Jack noticed Jeremy's confused expression. "A multicell cluster is a group of thunderstorms. A squall line is a line of thunderstorms."

Jack handed tuna mayonnaise sandwiches around. He explained the different lightning types.

"Keep an eye over there," he advised, pointing at a brooding cumulonimbus.

Sure enough, halfway through his third sandwich, Jeremy witnessed electric tentacles creeping across the cloud. With each brilliant, branchlike sprawl, he expected the Norse god Thor to step out and wield his hammer.

"Wow!" Jeremy gasped.

"Anvil crawlers," Barney sighed through his viewfinder. "Sensational."

Lightning Strikes!

Lightning is named according to whether it strikes the ground, the air or other clouds. Here are a few common types.

1. Intra-cloud lightning (IC)
This is lightning inside a cloud. There are often no lightning bolts, but the sky lights up.

2. Bolt from the blue
This is when lightning strikes the ground away from the storm cloud.

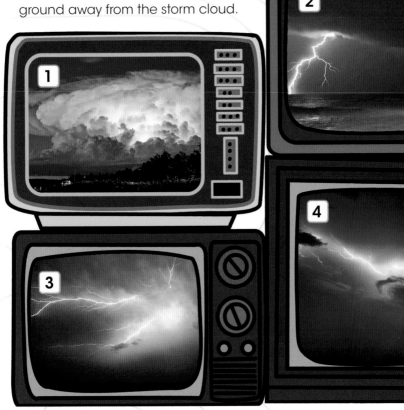

3. Cloud to air (CA)

This is lightning that comes from the top of a cloud and strikes the air.

4. Cloud to cloud (CC)

This is a lightning bolt that travels from one cloud to another.

5. Cloud to ground (CG)

This is the best-known type of lightning. It is when lightning strikes the ground.

6. Heat lightning

This is when lightning from a thunderstorm is too far away to be heard but is seen.

Weather Radar

Radar plays a sound into the air, and when the sound reaches an object, it bounces back. The time it takes for the sound to return gives the shape and distance of an object.

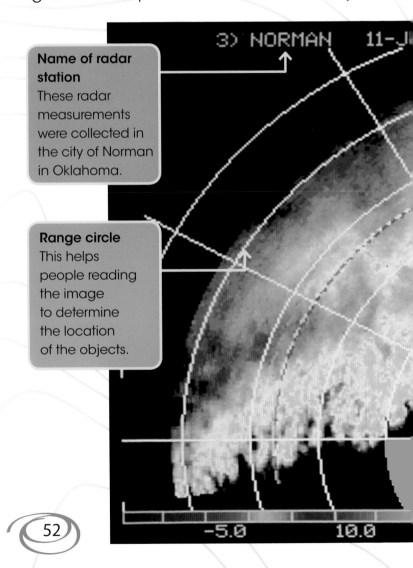

3> NORMAN   11-J

Name of radar station
These radar measurements were collected in the city of Norman in Oklahoma.

Range circle
This helps people reading the image to determine the location of the objects.

-5.0   10.0

Date and time
This indicates that readings were taken on 11 June, 1985, at 10.08 p.m. The time is in the 24-hour format.

Radial
This line works with the range circles to help scientists determine location.

Pixel
These are the tiny blocks that make up the image.

Squall line
This is a line of thunderstorms that often causes tornadoes to form. The bright-yellow colour shows that there is heavy rainfall in this area.

Product scale
The numbers and colours in the scale represent the levels of rain or snow on the image: the higher the number or brighter the colour, the more rain there is.

22:08:15 0.7° PPI DBZ.

200
160
120
80
330 40 30
300 60
270 90
240 120
210 180 150

0   40.0   55.0

Make Lightning!

If you cannot wait until a thunderstorm to see lightning, make it at home! It is easy to recreate the conditions for lightning yourself in just a few steps.

What you will need

aluminium pie pan   polystyrene tray   scissors   tape

Here is how to do it

1 Cut the corner off the polystyrene tray and tape it to the middle of the pie pan. This creates a handle so that you can move the pan without letting the charge escape.

2 Take the rest of the polystyrene tray and rub it on your hair quickly.

3 Being careful not to touch anything but the handle, pick up the aluminium pan and put it down on top of the polystyrene tray.

4 Turn off the lights and move your fingertip close to the pie pan slowly. Be careful not to touch the polystyrene tray. Watch for a tiny spark of lightning jumping from the pan to your finger.

What is happening

A flash of lightning occurs when negatively charged particles in clouds are attracted to positively charged particles in the ground. When you rubbed the tray against your hair, you picked up a negative charge. This charge was attracted to the positive charge in the pan, creating a spark.

The Making of a Supercell

The storm chasers lodged in a Paris motel that night. Everyone slept in fresh clothes to save time in the morning.

"Genius!" Jeremy thought. From now on, he would wear his school clothes to bed. "Could I get away with only brushing my teeth at night?" he thought to himself. "Not likely."

At dawn, they strolled to a 24-hour pancake house. Jack flung his cousin a banana.

"Tell your folks we fed you fruit!" he insisted.

When leaving town, they stopped by a replica Eiffel Tower for a souvenir photograph. Jeremy had been to Paris, France. He informed the storm chasers that the original tower did not wear a cowboy hat.

"This isn't the first Eiffel Tower in Paris, Texas," Barney remarked. "Guess what happened to the old one."

"Lightning strike?" Jeremy shrugged.

"Possibly," chuckled Barney. "Officially, a tornado tore it down."

"And we might see one today," added Flash.

Everyone spoke at once.

"GUYS!" shouted Jack. "Hop in the van. We're driving to Wichita!"

"With conditions forming for a supercell – that's a big, rotating thunderstorm – we won't be the only storm chasers in Kansas!" continued Jack.

Ryders on the Storm rocketed north along the Indian Nation Turnpike. As they approached Wichita, Flash stopped for petrol. Jeremy stepped out to stretch his legs. He steeled himself against the barrelling wind.

"What's the biggest twister to have hit Tornado Alley?" he asked.

Flash paused. "In May 2013, an EF5 tornado struck El Reno, Oklahoma," she explained sadly. "Tragically, 18 people were killed. That tornado was four kilometres wide."

Jeremy nodded. He now remembered the news reports.

Flash swiped her credit card on the pump.

"All tornadoes are terribly dangerous, Jeremy. An EF1 will overturn a caravan.

An EF2 will destroy it. If we improve our understanding of tornadoes, we can develop better warning systems. Then we can save more lives."

Jeremy now understood his cousins' obsession with the weather.

Jack wound down his window. "Dominator, due north!" he shouted, pointing frantically at the highway.

A bizarre dark-metal tank rumbled away in the distance. A convoy of SUVs followed.

"The circus is coming to town," Jack bellowed at Jeremy, "and kiddo, you're joining the circus!"

They hurtled down a dirt road, as wind and rain rocked the van. Flash skidded to a halt. There was no need to check the GPS. Ryders on the Storm had met their supercell. It seemed the entire storm-chasing community was crowded around this one Kansas farm.

Everyone watched the wall cloud roll in from the east.

It was a beast.

Jack frowned at the Doppler radar. "It's 14 kilometres away," he informed everyone. "The mesocyclone is around three kilometres in diameter. That's the part in the centre of the supercell that rotates. Time will tell if it sprouts a tornado."

The storm chasers' mobiles beeped in a frantic chorus. Jeremy jumped.

"Wireless Emergency Alert," Suze explained calmly. "It's a government tornado warning."

Jeremy watched anxiously as the family who lived on the farm fled to a storm shelter. The sky was a sickly shade of green. Flash spoke on a two-way radio. When she switched off, she turned to Jeremy.

"That was Dominator's support crew. If a tornado drops, Dominator will move in and intercept it – that means drive into it. Can you believe that?"

Right now, Jeremy could not believe his eyes…

A wisp stretched from the rolling cloud, forming an angry claw. It pointed menacingly towards the ground. For the first time, Jeremy noticed a row of yellow devices planted in the fields.

"Doppler on Wheels have laid pods in its path!" Barney whooped, excitedly ruffling Jeremy's hair.

The storm chasers stared out of the windscreen and windows, spellbound. Jack could barely contain himself. "Have we got touchdown? Have we got touchdown?" he chanted.

"Is it a t-tornado?" Jeremy stammered.

"Funnel cloud," Suze muttered, clicking away. "If it hits the ground, it's a tornado."

Then, as magically as it had arrived, the 'claw' wisped into nothing. Jack sank his head in his hands and groaned. For one odd moment, the van was silent. Flash winked at Jeremy.

"Still pretty impressive, right?" she said.

Jeremy tried to grin, but instead clenched his teeth. It sounded like someone was hammering the roof. "Thor?" he thought to himself, remembering the Norse god of thunder.

Jack wildly pointed at the windscreen. Ice ping-ponged all over it.

"Ready for the next piece of action, Jeremy?" he grinned. Jack Ryder recovered quickly from disappointment.

As hail pummelled the van, Jeremy felt like he was Han Solo flying the Millennium Falcon into an asteroid field. Jeremy was *very* imaginative. Flash noticed Jeremy's serious 'Han' look.

"Don't worry," she smiled. "Hailstorms rarely last more than 15 minutes."

Jack dug out the gym bag full of balls.

"Take your pick!" he announced. "Guess the size of the biggest hailstone you're going to find."

"Golf ball!" ventured Suze.

"Basketball!" joked Barney.

Jeremy quietly slid a ball into his pocket.

When the hail eventually passed, they examined the icy carpet glistening over the farmland. It was enchanting.

QUESTION:
Use your imagination, too. What would driving through a hailstorm be like?

"Beautiful, right?" Flash smiled. Her face grew glum as the people who lived on the farm emerged from the storm shelter. "Sadly, hail can destroy crops."

Jeremy hadn't thought of that.

"Check this out!" called a storm chaser from a neighbouring van. She held up an enormous hailstone for Jeremy to inspect.

"What do you think?" she asked.

Jeremy removed the battered cricket ball from his pocket. It was the same size!

Ryders on the Storm stopped by Clarabelle's Steakhouse for dinner. Jeremy learned it was a storm chaser hangout.

The Fujita Scale

The Enhanced Fujita Scale is used to rate tornado intensity. Meteorologists assign categories EF0 to EF5 based on the amount of damage.

Category	Wind speed	
	mph	km/h
EF0	65–85	105–137
EF1	86–110	138–177
EF2	111–135	178–217
EF3	136–165	218–266
EF4	166–200	267–322
EF5	Over 200	Over 322

What tornadoes can do

EF0 Chimneys will be damaged, tree branches broken and shallow-rooted trees toppled.

EF1 Roof surfaces will be peeled off, windows broken and some tree trunks snapped.

EF2 Roof structures will be damaged and large trees snapped or uprooted.

EF3 Roofs will be torn away, some small buildings destroyed and most trees uprooted.

EF4 Well-built houses will be destroyed and cars blown over some distance.

EF5 Houses will be lifted from foundations and reinforced concrete structures damaged.

Storm-chasing Vehicle

Storm chasers need vehicles that can keep •
with fast-moving storms. Most vehicles are
managed by the Center of Severe Weather
Research (CSWR) or the National Oceanic
and Atmospheric Administration (NOAA).

Doppler on Wheels

Operator: CSWR

Gear: radar

Features: serves as
a mobile radar station

Tornado Intercept Vehicle

Operator: Sean Casey

Gear: IMAX camera

Features: body armour
to drive into tornadoes

Lockheed WP-3D Orion

Operator: NOAA
Gear: radar
Features: flies into storms
to take measurements

Mesonet vehicle

Operator: various
Features: carries all
the instruments of
a weather station

Gulfstream IV-SP

Operator: NOAA
Gear: pressure sensors
Features: flies around
storms taking readings

Field command unit

Operator: CSWR
Gear: computers
Features: collects and
processes weather data

Storm Forecast

Gerald: We've been hearing reports of some severe weather passing through western Texas and Oklahoma. It looks like some of it may be moving our way. We'll hear now from Becky Storm, our meteorologist. Becky, how's it looking?

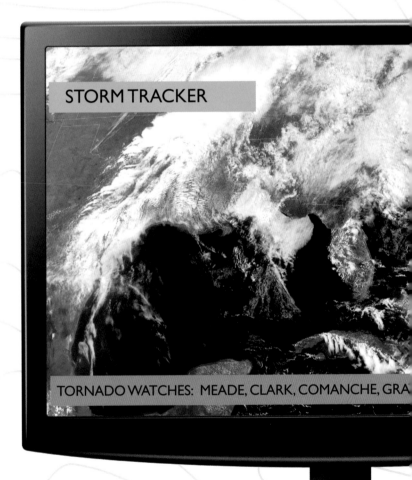

STORM TRACKER

TORNADO WATCHES: MEADE, CLARK, COMANCHE, GRA

Becky: Well, Gerald, we've been keeping an eye on some very active weather here. Taking a look at our satellite view, we can see a lot of storm activity moving through southern Kansas. These are the ingredients that produce tornadoes. We've had severe thunderstorms with heavy rain and strong winds throughout the southeast and the Great Plains.

ORD, KIOWA, EDWARDS

In western Texas and southern Oklahoma, there have been some tornadoes already in the last 24 hours.

In northern Oklahoma, we have reports of giant hailstones, and even a few funnel clouds.

Overnight, these storms will move over into the Dodge City area. Expect some damaging wind and hail.

Then tomorrow, tornadoes are looking very likely, so tornado watches are in effect.

How Hail Forms

Hail is a kind of precipitation – like rain or snow – that is in the form of solid ice. This is how it forms.

1. Hailstones start life as frozen water droplets or snow pellets called hail embryos.

2. The powerful air currents in a cumulonimbus cloud carry the hail embryo up and down.

3. At the bottom of the cloud, the hail embryo becomes covered in a layer of moisture that freezes as the hail embryo whirls upwards.

4. At the top of the cloud, the hail embryo is covered in a layer of ice.

5. The hail embryo gets bigger and bigger until it is so heavy, it drops to the ground as a hailstone.

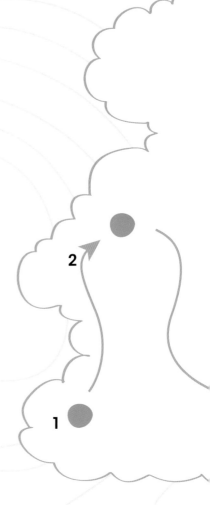

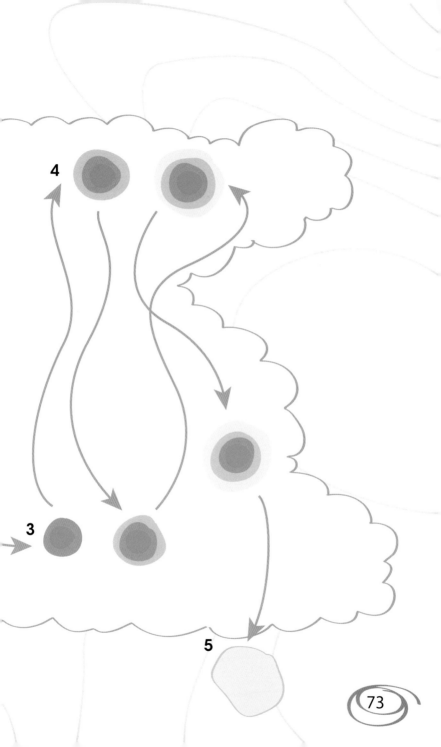

Disaster Strikes

The parking lot looked like a meteorology exhibit. Inside the restaurant, everyone was eager to share hair-raising tales. Jeremy thought if he saw another funnel cloud, his hair would lift off his head!

They stayed in caravans and rose early the next day. After a big breakfast, Flash called co-workers at the Storm Prediction Centre.

"Storm activity is headed towards Bethany, Oklahoma this afternoon," she advised.

Jack was driving. "Let's take the back roads," he said. "I'm tired of the Interstate."

For over four hours, they passed flattened wheat fields. Until yesterday, the fields had been ready for harvest.

Jack slammed on the brakes. The van juddered to a stop.

"Darn it!" he shouted.

A swollen creek ran like a torrent where the road should have been. Everyone leapt out of the van.

"With the crest in the road, I almost didn't see it," Jack said, dismayed. "It could have killed us!"

They all stared. They were speechless.

While Barney and Jack set up traffic cones, Flash called Highway Patrol to alert them of the danger. Suze, who was trained in first aid, checked to see if anyone was injured in the sudden brake. After everyone had calmed down, Barney and Suze began filming and taking pictures.

When the police arrived to secure the scene, the storm chasers climbed back in the van. Flash was now at the wheel. They wanted the quickest route to Bethany. Unfortunately, the only way there was a maze of dirt roads. Everywhere they looked, the storm had been there first.

It was a gloomy excursion: metal roofs peeled from farm buildings like lids on tins of sardines. Cars lay scattered on roadsides. The windows and windscreens were riddled with holes from hailstones. They looked like something from old gangster films.

Saddest of all, a group of cows lay lifeless against a wire fence.

Barney winced when he saw Jeremy's horrified expression.

"Lightning must have struck the fence," he explained gently. "It would have been quick."

After a murmured conversation with Flash, Jack turned and addressed everyone in the back of the van.

"Listen," he said, "thanks to these back roads, we're still a long way from anywhere. Let's scratch the chase in Bethany and start fresh tomorrow."

"You'll get no argument from us," said Barney. "Right?"

"Right!" agreed Suze and Jeremy.

Five kilometres further down the road, they slowed before a small farmhouse. It had suffered severe storm damage. Oddly, its rusty mailbox was still standing.

The family were clearing debris strewn across their garden. Flash veered into the driveway and parked. She went over to speak to them.

Then Ryders on the Storm were handed five rubbish bags and five pairs of rubber gloves.

The youngest boy, Tom, examined the van.

"Are you storm chasers?" he marvelled. "Do you drive into twisters like on TV?"

"Don't be silly, Tom!" smiled his mother. Then she inspected the van more closely. She raised her eyebrows. "Well, maybe they do…"

"We are storm chasers," Flash chuckled, "but we don't intercept tornadoes."

> **QUESTION:**
> If you were a storm chaser, what role would you take?

As they bundled rubbish in the garden, the Joneses explained what had happened the night before.

"A tornado warning was issued, and I was at home with the kids preparing dinner," Sarah Jones said. "So we ran to our shelter. There was no twister, luckily, but then we came out to no electricity and all this mess."

"I was driving home from a friend's farm," added her husband Bob. "I weathered the storm, but then came the hail. You can see what happened…"

Bob pointed grimly at his brand-new pickup truck.

"More holes than Swiss cheese on a golf course," muttered Jeremy, a bit too loudly.

The other storm chasers shot him looks darker than a cumulonimbus. Jeremy felt embarrassed. Then the Joneses began to chuckle and belly laugh.

"Thanks, kid. We really needed that!" hooted Bob, slapping Jeremy on the back.

A couple of hours later, the storm chasers departed. To help make things clearer, the Joneses had drawn directions to the Interstate on their 'emergency' paper map. Jeremy rested in the van and his eyelids grew heavy.

Jeremy jolted awake. What time was it? Two power company trucks that had stopped to repair damaged electricity cables blocked the road. Jack threw the van into reverse, but it made a weird noise. FLUB! FLUB! FLUB-FLUB-FLUB! He leapt out to investigate.

"Darn it!" he shouted. "Two flat tyres!" he groaned. "With only one spare!"

Everyone grumbled. Flash pointed past the electricians. There, in neon lights, was an enormous blinking pizza. Next door was a garage.

"Forget tyres! Operation: Pizza!" Flash commanded like an army general.

Once inside, Flash asked the owner, Jim, what had happened. He said the storm had brought down power lines. Jim was the town's pizza chef and its mechanic.

After dishing up delicious pepperoni pizzas, he fixed both punctures. "Eight-centimetre roofing nails," he explained. "Great for roofs, bad for tyres."

That night, with no other accommodation around, Ryders on the Storm camped in Jim's pizza restaurant. After dinner, they toasted marshmallows in the wood-fired oven.

As Jeremy drifted to sleep, he realised he was no longer jealous of his parents' holiday in Fiji.

QUESTION:
Consider the pros and cons for each holiday. Which would you prefer?

Start here

Hail
Foiled on your first roll! You have been hit by a hailstorm. Go back a space.

Go forwards one space!

A GAME OF HAZARDS

Landslides

A landslide has blocked the road. Miss a turn.

Go forwards one space!

Go forwards two spaces!

Flooding
A flash flood has blocked the roads. Miss a turn.

You will need two or more people, a die and a counter each. Take turns rolling the die and moving clockwise around the board. The winner is the first player to make it around.

Go forwards one space!

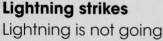

Lightning strikes
Lightning is not going to stop you! Roll again.

Flat tyre
You need to stop and change a flat tyre. Miss a turn.

Tornado History

Tornadoes have always been wreaking havoc in the USA. Here are some of the most significant events.

St. Louis–East St. Louis Tornado
Category: EF4
Area hit: St. Louis, Missouri

Tupelo–Gainesville Outbreak
Area hit: Mississippi, Georgia
Number of tornadoes: 12
Fact: this was the second-deadliest outbreak in US history.

1913

1925

1896

1936

The Tri-State Tornado
Category: EF5
Area hit: Missouri to Indiana
Fact: it was the deadliest tornado in US history.

Omaha, Nebraska

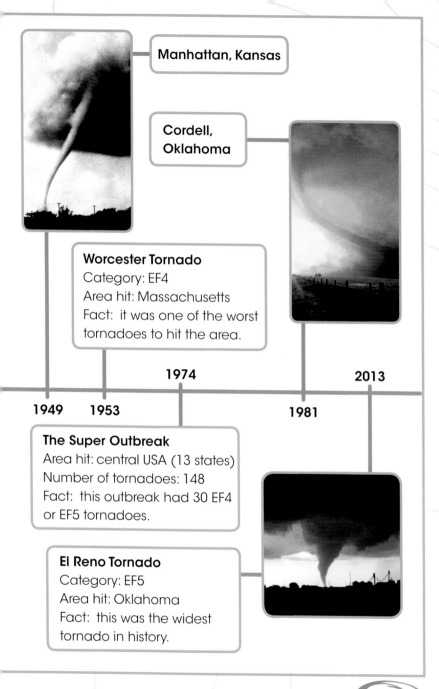

Manhattan, Kansas

Cordell, Oklahoma

Worcester Tornado
Category: EF4
Area hit: Massachusetts
Fact: it was one of the worst tornadoes to hit the area.

1974

2013

1949   1953

1981

The Super Outbreak
Area hit: central USA (13 states)
Number of tornadoes: 148
Fact: this outbreak had 30 EF4 or EF5 tornadoes.

El Reno Tornado
Category: EF5
Area hit: Oklahoma
Fact: this was the widest tornado in history.

Boom or Bust?

Jeremy awoke to the smell of pizza. Breakfast pizza! While the others snoozed, Jim taught him how to spin the dough. Like a floury disc, the dough escaped from Jeremy's hands and flung onto Barney's face. FLUMP! Barney sat up in his sleeping bag, confused. Jim and Jeremy burst out laughing. Barney looked like an Egyptian mummy rising from his sarcophagus.

After enjoying Jim's breakfast, Ryders on the Storm hooked up their computers. Flash explained the day's chase to Jeremy.

"We have a storm headed towards Dodge City that has developed a 'hook echo' shape. This area in the hook is a 'mesocyclone'. That's the rotating updraft of wind. Warm moist air is sucked in on the right of the mesocyclone. We call that the 'inflow notch'. If a tornado forms, it will be under the mesocyclone. The tornado will travel in the same direction as the inflow notch. Make sense?"

Jeremy went cross-eyed.

"Sure, but will we see a tornado?" he asked.

Flash crossed her fingers and her eyes.
"We might!"

QUESTION:
How would you feel if you were about to see a tornado?

Four hours later, west of Dodge City, Kansas, Jeremy felt like he had met a ghost. There, 10 kilometres away, was a giant wedge-shaped tornado. His feet were so sweaty from fear, they slid in his socks!

"We're calling this in!" Jack shouted.

Today, Ryders on the Storm were the only storm chasers around. Jack alerted the National Weather Service with the coordinates and estimated size of the tornado.

"It's approximately two kilometres wide and is travelling on an eastward path," he advised. "The immediate region isn't populated – just a few grain silos and farm buildings. No houses."

Flash gunned the engine as if she were a race car driver.

"We're headed west!" she hollered enthusiastically. "Fast!"

"Wow, look at that motion! Strong rotation!" Barney marvelled through his viewfinder.

"It's a hungry beast!" Suze added, clicking her camera.

Jeremy gulped as the tornado ploughed through a barn, chomping it to bits. He did not know what to say. He could not look away. No matter how fast Flash drove, the tornado grew bigger and bigger.

Bzzzzzzz! Bzzzzzzz! Bzzzzzzz! Jeremy pulled his mobile from his pocket. It was his parents.

"Hello?" he answered.

"Jeremy? Is that you, darling?" It was his mother. She sounded very relaxed.

"Yes, Mum. I'm here. How's Fiji?" Jeremy replied casually.

"Hot!" she laughed. "What's the weather like over there?"

Jeremy eyed the enormous tornado wreaking havoc out his window. It seemed to be getting closer, rather than further away. The noise enveloped the van like a rumbling steam train.

"Oh, it's a little windy out!" he shouted.

"Are you at a railway station, Jeremy? What is that sound?" his mum asked.

"No… uh… um…" Jeremy replied, making absolutely no sense.

"I beg your pardon, sweetheart? I can't hear above that racket!"

"Yup, just hanging out in the Wild, Wild West!"

Jeremy tried to act normally. He was not a good actor.

"What?" his mum said sharply. Then she sounded worried. "Jeremy, is everything okay over there?"

"Everything is great, Mum. I love you!" he shouted.

Flash smashed through a wooden fence. They passed concerned cows and horses. Jeremy thought he would never speak to his mother again.

"I love you too, darling!" she shouted.

Jeremy hung up.

"North, sis, north!" Jack directed, waving ahead.

Flash rammed her foot on the accelerator. Soggy bales of hay rained from the skies, bouncing off the windscreen.

"Ever dressed up as a haystack?" she snorted grimly.

Nobody laughed.

"The tornado just backed on to itself," Jack observed gravely. "It is headed right for us."

Jeremy stared at the whirling monster behind them. As they ploughed through the swampy field, he was grateful for the heavy-terrain tyres on the van.

"How far away is it?" he gasped.

"Three kilometres," Barney replied. His jaws were clenched.

Up ahead was a sweeping vista filled with wind turbines.

"A wind farm?" Suze shouted in despair. "We are not driving into that. Not with a tornado!"

As she spoke, a bolt of lightning shot from the clouds and struck a manically whirring blade. Jagged branches of blue-white light arced along a row of turbines. It looked like an experiment in a mad professor's laboratory.

"We are not driving into that!" Flash agreed.

She swiftly veered left. She had found a road to follow. It was pitted with very deep potholes. BUMP! BUMP! BUMP!

Jeremy turned to see the tornado tagging monstrously behind them. It shredded the road and gobbled it in its whirring vortex. Suze was right when she called it a hungry beast.

Flash slammed on the brakes. There was a diversion sign: 'Danger! Cliff! Dead end ahead!' Were they trapped?

"Look!" Jack pointed.

Jeremy's eyes followed Jack's finger out of the window. The twister had sharply changed course. His mouth gaped as he watched it tear into the wind farm and pluck turbines from the ground like toothpicks.

Suddenly, it seemed to run out of puff.

"It's getting ropey!" Flash exclaimed.

The 'wedge' got thinner and thinner. It seemed to be dwindling into nothing.

"It's going!" shouted Barney.

"It's going!" shouted Suze.

"It's gone!" shouted Jack.

Jeremy could not believe it. There were no high-fives or cheers. Everyone sat and stared, speechless. That had been a very close call.

Jack broke the eerie silence by suggesting they swing by Dodge City for some 'ordinary' sightseeing.

"What? No driving over cliffs to escape killer tornadoes?" Jeremy replied drily.

Flash grinned at Jeremy sheepishly in the rearview mirror. "It's probably best we leave that to cartoon characters," she said.

Jack reached into his gym bag and pulled out a Ryders on the Storm baseball jacket. He presented it to Jeremy.

"Epic!" Jeremy shouted. "Thanks!"

"You really earned your stripes today," Jack smiled.

Flash had driven barely a kilometre before slamming on the brakes. Wordlessly, she pointed ahead. Jeremy froze. Was it another tornado?

Everyone scrambled out of the van. Instead of scanning the skies, they looked down. The road was a mess! Great chunks of

asphalt were missing or smashed like a china vase. It was the same road the tornado had chased them down. Jeremy got goose pimples. Thank goodness Flash drove as fast as her namesake. Imagine if her parents had called her Snail!

QUESTION:
If you were reporting on the devastation shown in the picture below, what words would you use?

KANSAS

TORNADO DEVASTATES RURAL COMMUNITY

Dodge City, Kansas – A devastating tornado tore through a rural community in southern Kansas yesterday.

The twister measured EF4 on the Enhanced Fujita Scale, the second-highest level. It flattened entire neighbourhoods, with winds of up to 275 km/h (170 mph). Scientists said it was 185 m (600 feet) wide.

HERALD

In spite of tremendous damage to property, there is great relief that there have been no fatalities. About 40 people are being treated in hospitals for minor injuries.

The storm destroyed several areas, leaving piles of ruined buildings and broken wood, overturned and crushed cars and fires.

Survivor Tom Sunshine said, "Our front garden looks like a rubbish heap. There are piles of glass and wood thrown all over the neighbourhood. Some homes are completely gone. It's really devastating."

The first tornado warning was issued at about 2.40 p.m. local time. It hit 48 km (30 miles) southeast of Dodge City at 3.01 p.m. and remained on the ground for about 45 minutes, leaving a trail of destruction about 32 km (20 miles) long.

Kansas Governor Sarah Hanson said, "Wednesday was a sad day. Nothing can return what has been lost, but we'll do everything we possibly can to help those affected to recover as quickly as possible."

Another local resident, Sarah Gilbert, said, "I'm just happy that I was able to find my son and that my family is OK. The scene in the neighbourhood is just totally catastrophic."

Tornadoes, hail and high winds also hit western Texas and Oklahoma.

Weird Weather

Sometimes the weather does *really* crazy things, which cannot always be explained. Here are a few of the world's weirdest weather events.

Ice bombs

Ice bombs are giant hailstones that are sometimes rumoured to fall even when there is no storm!

Firenado

This occurs when a tornado combines with a wild fire. The winds pick up the fire, creating a fiery vortex.

Upward lightning
Sometimes lightning can actually appear to come from the ground. Scientists are not sure exactly how this happens.

Raining frogs and fish
Some people have reported raining animals. Scientists think they may have been lifted into the air by tornadoes.

Waterspouts
When a tornado occurs over water, the wind sucks up the water. This is a waterspout.

Great Plains Tours

Come and enjoy the many wondrous sites of the Great Plains! Our qualified tour guides provide a range of tailor-made tours to some of our region's most interesting attractions.

Oklahoma City
Old and new come together in this buzzing metropolis. Giddyup to the National Cowboy Museum for a bit of local history, or marvel at the futuristic Gold Dome, a convention centre with a roof made of 625 aluminium panels.

Tailor your holiday

Destination

▼

Holiday duration

▼

Number of people

▼

Search >

Storm-chasing tours

Oklahoma................>

Texas......................>

Kansas....................>

Nebraska.................>

Dinosaur Valley

Walk in the footsteps of dinosaurs in Texas's Dinosaur Valley State Park. Here you will find some of the world's best-preserved dinosaur tracks. You can also explore the park's range of beautiful flora and fauna on foot, by bike or on horseback.

Paris

Welcome to Paris – Texas, that is! It may look like its French sister, but this Eiffel Tower has some Texas charm. Take a picture in front of one of North America's favourite pit stops, before enjoying a meal at one of the eateries near the Plaza downtown.

Wichita

Explore the lifestyle of the Kiowa, Cheyenne, Lakota and other Great Plains Native American tribes at the Mid-America All-Indian Centre, or get an introduction to living like a cowboy at the Old Cowtown Museum.

Dodge City

You will think you have stepped back in time to the Old West at Dodge City's Boot Hill Museum. Come in July or August for a rootin' tootin' good time at Dodge City Days and Rodeo, complete with barbecues and rodeo clowns.

One Last Twist?

Jeremy moped. Saying goodbye to Barney and Suze back in Oklahoma City was tough. He had never had such an action-packed week with anyone! He felt like they were his very old friends.

"Mate, as soon as I've taken a nap and had a shower, I'll start editing the chase footage," Barney reassured him.

"I bet my edited DVD gets to your house in England before you do!"

Suze gave Jeremy a big hug.

"I'll send you my best pictures," she promised. "There weren't any UFO clouds, but that tornado was something from out of this world, wasn't it?"

"Intergalactic," Jeremy agreed flatly. "Can you blow that one up, poster size?"

"Well, I could," she laughed, "but do you really want such a hefty reminder?"

Jeremy whistled.

"You're right, Suze," he replied, brightening. "I would never get a good night's sleep. Just send me a poster of your nicest, fluffiest cloud!"

Suze promised she would.

The tornado near Dodge City had rated EF4 on the Enhanced Fujita scale. Ryders on the Storm had been very lucky to escape that day.

Back at Jack and Flash's house, Jeremy's eyes bugged out at the TV. Out of 118 channels, he had switched on *The Wizard of Oz*. It was the scene where the twister hit Aunt Em and Uncle Henry's farm. "How weird!" he thought.

Hedgehog buried his head under Jeremy's leg and whimpered. He was not a storm chaser like the humans of the household.

"It's only a film, Hedge," Jeremy chuckled, ruffling his dark, smooth coat. "A very old film."

It was Jeremy's last day in Oklahoma City. His bag was packed and waiting beside the front door, ready to leave for the airport. He could not believe that his holiday was over so soon. Never before had so much happened in such a short space of time.

In his lap was a bowl of peach pie, hot from the oven. It was just as delicious as on the first night when he had arrived. Jack walked in the room, frowning at his mobile.

"Jeremy, I just missed a call from Fiji," he said. "You'd better listen to the message."

Jeremy took the mobile from his cousin. It was his mother.

"Hi Jack, it's Lauren. Have you heard about Cyclone Mona? It's passing by Fiji but not expected to hit. The airport is closed, so we can't leave. Please call me soon and I'll explain."

Jeremy's mind was in a whir. It suddenly seemed that he was not headed back to London! Would his parents be okay? He looked at his cousins, confused.

"What's a cyclone?" he asked. "Is that the same thing as a tornado?"

Flash shook her head. "Cyclones form over the sea's surface," she explained, "in warm tropical areas above 26 degrees Celsius – places like Fiji."

"In Australia and Oceania, they refer to large-scale storms that form over tropical waters as cyclones," Jack added. "Here in the States, we call these storms hurricanes. In Asia, they are known as typhoons."

Jeremy nodded quietly.

"Are cyclones over and done with quickly, like tornadoes?" he asked.

Flash shook her head.

"I'm sorry, Jeremy," she said grimly. "Cyclones can rage for many days."

Jack and Flash returned to the office the next morning. Jeremy joined them as the 'intern'. Checking in with the Australian Bureau of Meteorology radars, they anxiously watched Tropical Cyclone Mona whirl an erratic path over the South Pacific. It lasted three days. The cyclone was downgraded to a storm as it reached the cool waters near New Zealand.

Jack and Flash launched a bunch of weather balloons to celebrate. As the balloons drifted towards the upper atmosphere, Jeremy received a phone call from his parents. Nadi International Airport had opened. It was time to go home.

"What a holiday!" his dad sighed. "Jeremy, you would not believe the ordeal we have been through."

Jeremy smiled to himself. He could not wait to show his mum and dad Barney's DVD when it arrived.

His father cleared his throat.

"So, what was the weather like in Oklahoma City? Your mother mentioned it was windy. I hope you packed a jumper."

"That's right, Dad," Jeremy chuckled quietly. "It got a bit windy."

At Will Rogers World Airport the next day, Jeremy hugged his cousins.

"Well, this holiday has certainly been an experience," he sighed happily. "When I arrived, I was determined to read books, watch TV and mind my own business."

"I'm sorry our storm-chasing adventure ruined your thrilling plans!" he shouted.

"Jack," Jeremy said quietly, "you shout a lot. Did anyone ever tell you that?"

"Never! Ever! Ever!" Jack shouted.

"Always!" Flash nodded vigorously.

Jeremy laughed. It was cool to be related to twin meteorologist storm chasers.

"You know what? I might go solo on this storm-chasing gig!" he announced. "London did have tornadoes in 2006!"

"Maybe you could chase storms on the bus?" Flash suggested.

Lightning erupted in the sky. KRRRRAAAAAAKKKKKKKAAAAKKKK!

Jeremy cast a very nervous look at his plane waiting at the gate.

"You know what?" he said. "I always prefer taking the bus."

Anatomy of a Tornado

Warm, moist air rushes up into a big thundercloud supercell and rubs against cold air higher up. The two air masses turn around each other and create a wide column of revolving air. This column spins faster and faster as it sucks in more warm air. This creates a tornado.

Tornado hitting a town

Tornado above town

Tornado hitting town

Tornado destroying buildings

Warm air rushes in

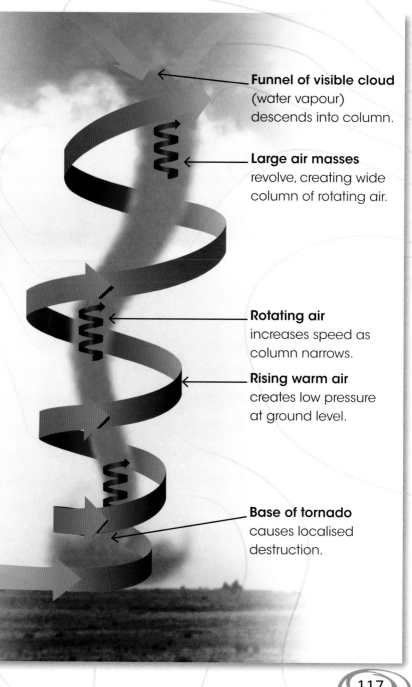

Funnel of visible cloud (water vapour) descends into column.

Large air masses revolve, creating wide column of rotating air.

Rotating air increases speed as column narrows.

Rising warm air creates low pressure at ground level.

Base of tornado causes localised destruction.

About me

I'm Jeremy, a regular London boy who loves cooking and eating! I write about things I've eaten, things I'm making, food experiments and any other adventures along the way.

Blog archive

Eat This!

My Food Experiments and Other Adventures

You won't believe the adventure I've had. This was a real adventure. A few weeks ago, I went to visit my cousins Jack and Flash in Oklahoma, in the USA.

They're meteorologists. So, what's so exciting about that? Well, they're not just any meteorologists — they're storm chasers!

They travel around central USA — an area called 'Tornado Alley' — looking for tornadoes. So I spent the whole trip driving around Oklahoma, Texas and Kansas looking for tornadoes with them and their friends Suze and Barney.

I'm not ashamed to admit that I was terrified the entire time. From the very beginning, we were coming face-to-face with crazy lightning, gigantic hailstones and extreme thunderstorms.

We drove around for a long time before we finally got close to a tornado. I could see the winds picking up everything in sight and tossing it around. I saw cars flipped over and roofs torn off houses.

When the tornado died down, we started to head back to Oklahoma. On the way, we stopped by a house that had been destroyed by the tornado. It was a truly humbling sight. The family that lived there had lost everything, although, thankfully, none of them was hurt. I really admired them. I don't think I would have held it together so well.

The whole thing was an amazing experience. I'm really glad I went and got to hang out with Jack and Flash. There was one other awesome thing about the trip. I had the best peach pie, pancakes and pizza in my life! I'm going to ask Flash and Jack for some recipes, and I'll post them here so you can taste them for yourselves!

Well, I guess that's pretty much it. I hope you won't be too bored by my future posts now that you've heard all about my latest adventures!

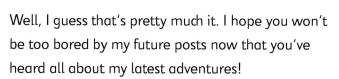

Tornado Shape Poem

A shape poem is a poem that is shaped like the thing it describes. The shape adds to the meaning of the poem.

To write a shape poem, it helps to start by writing down all the words that come to mind about the chosen topic. These words can then be used in the poem.

gusts

spinning

clouds

roaring

vortex

thunder

roofs

twister

tornado

vacuum cleaner

lightning

rotating

destruction

storms

dust

winds

air

hail

picking up
everything
in its path

merry-go-round

In a twist

We felt the rain, wind and hail, and

Then the thunder and lightning came.

The winds gathered up and began to spin

Like a spinning top, sucking up dust like a vacuum cleaner.

The twister went round and round, like a merry-go-round.

The gusts of air were picking up dust.

It continued to roar loudly,

Destroying everything

Along the way.

Soon it was

Gone.

Storm-chasing Quiz

Were you paying attention? See if you can remember the answers to these questions about what you have read.

 1. On average, how many tornadoes hit the USA each year?

 2. According to the Ryders, during which hurricane did their stormy arrival take place?

 3. Which storm chaser is known for having created a tornado in his home laboratory?

 4. Tornado Alley lies between which two North American mountain ranges?

 5. What does Suze do on the Ryders' storm-chasing trips?

 6. What kind of cloud is associated with thunderstorms and tornadoes?

 7. What is lightning that strikes the ground called?

 8. According to Flash, which was the biggest tornado to have hit Tornado Alley?

9. What does Flash say the Dominator will do if the tornado drops?

10. According to Suze, when does a funnel cloud become a tornado?

11. What kind of ball is the same size as the largest hailstone that Ryders on the Storm see?

12. What is the most powerful category of tornado on the Enhanced Fujita Scale?

13. What do Ryders on the Storm decide to do when they see the Joneses' damaged farmhouse?

14. What does the tornado near Dodge City do to the wind turbines?

15. What are cyclones called in the USA and in Asia?

Answers on page 125.

Glossary

anemometer
An instrument for recording the speed and direction of winds.

barometric pressure
The force of air pressing down on the ground or any other horizontal surface.

casualty
A person who is injured or killed.

cyclone
A violent tropical storm in the South Pacific.

deadbolt
A type of lock that is secured manually rather than automatically.

Doppler radar
A type of radar that tracks the movement of objects.

fauna
The animal life of an area.

flora
The plant life of an area.

funnel cloud
A funnel-shaped cloud with a rotating column of air.

Global Positioning System (GPS)
A system that provides location and time information using satellites in space.

meteorology
The study of the Earth's atmosphere, of the ways in which weather forms, and of methods of forecasting the weather.

pioneer
A person who helps to develop new ideas.

pre-designated
Chosen beforehand.

Index

Answers to the Storm-chasing Quiz

1. 1,253; **2.** Hurricane Hugo; **3.** Neil B. Ward;
4. The Rockies and the Appalachian Mountains;
5. She 'collects' clouds by photographing them;
6. Cumulonimbus; **7.** Cloud to ground (CG) lightning
8. The El Reno tornado in May 2013; **9.** It will intercept, or drive, into, it; **10.** When it hits the ground;
11. Cricket ball; **12.** EF5; **13.** Help the Joneses clean up;
14. It plucks them from the ground 'like toothpicks';
15. Hurricanes and typhoons.

Guide for Parents

DK Reads is a three-level interactive reading adventure series for children, developing the habit of reading widely for both pleasure and information. These chapter books have an exciting main narrative interspersed with a range of reading genres to suit your child's reading ability, as required by the National Curriculum. Each book is designed to develop your child's reading skills, fluency, grammar awareness and comprehension in order to build confidence and engagement when reading.

Ready for a *Reading Alone* book

YOUR CHILD SHOULD

- be able to read independently and silently for extended periods of time.
- read aloud flexibly and fluently, in expressive phrases with the listener in mind.
- respond to what he/she is reading with an enquiring mind.

A VALUABLE AND SHARED READING EXPERIENCE

Supporting children when they are reading proficiently can encourage them to value reading and to view reading as an interesting, purposeful and enjoyable pastime. So here are a few tips on how to use this book with your child.

TIP 1 Reading aloud as a learning opportunity:

- if your child has already read some of the book, ask him/her to explain the earlier part briefly.
- encourage your child to read slightly more slowly than his/her normal silent reading speed so that the words are clear and the listener has time to absorb the information, too.

Reading aloud provides your child with practice in expressive reading and performing to a listener, as well as a chance to share his/her responses to the storyline and the information.

TIP 2 Praise, share and chat:

- encourage your child to recall specific details after each chapter.

- provide opportunities for your child to pick out interesting words and discuss what they mean.

- discuss how the author captures the reader's interest, or how effective the non-fiction layouts are.

- ask the questions provided on some pages and in the quiz. These help to develop comprehension skills and awareness of the language used.

- ask if there's anything that your child would like to discover more about.

Further information can be researched in the index of other non-fiction books or on the Internet.

A FEW ADDITIONAL TIPS

- Continue to read to your child regularly to demonstrate fluency, phrasing and expression; to find out or check information; and for sharing enjoyment.

- Encourage your child to read a range of different genres, such as newspapers, poems, review articles and instructions.

- Provide opportunities for your child to read to a variety of eager listeners, such as a sibling or a grandparent.

Series consultant **Shirley Bickler** is a longtime advocate of carefully crafted, enthralling texts for young readers. Her LIFT initiative for infant teaching was the model for the National Literacy Strategy Literacy Hour, and she is co-author of *Book Bands for Guided Reading* published by Reading Recovery based at the Institute of Education.

Here are some other
DK Reads you might enjoy.

Terrors of the Deep
Marine biologists Dom and Jake take their deep-sea
submersible down into the world's deepest, darkest ocean
trench, the Mariana Trench.

Pony Club
Emma is so excited – she is going to
horseback-riding camp with her older sister!

Clash of the Gladiators
Travel back in time to ancient Rome when gladiators
entertained the crowds – will they be spared death?

The Mummy's Curse
Are our intrepid time travellers cursed? Experience ancient
Egyptian life along the banks of the Nile with them.

Ballet Academy
Lucy follows her dream as she trains to be a professional
dancer at the Academy. Will she make it through?

Galactic Mission
Year 2098: planet Earth is dying. Five school children embark
on a life or death mission to the distant star system of Alpha
Centauri to find a new home.

In the Shadow of the Volcano
Volcanologist Rosa Carelli and her son Carlo are caught up in
the dramatic events unfolding as Mount Vesuvius re-awakens.